Owlkids Books acknowledges the financial support of the Canada Council for the Arts, the Ontario Arts Council, the Government of Canada through the Canada Book Fund (CBF) and the Government of Ontario through the Ontario Media Development Corporation's Book Initiative for our publishing activities.

Published in Canada by
Owlkids Books Inc.
10 Lower Spadina Avenue
Toronto, ON M5V 2Z2

Published in the United States by
Owlkids Books Inc.
1700 Fourth Street
Berkeley, CA 94710

Library and Archives Canada Cataloguing in Publication

Whamond, Dave, author, illustrator
Frank and Laverne / by Dave Whamond and Jennifer Stokes ; illustrations by Dave Whamond.

Contents printed back-to-back and inverted.

ISBN 978-1-77147-145-9 (bound)

I. Stokes, Jennifer, author II. Title.

PS8645.H34F73 2016 jC813'.6 C2015-905420-6

Library of Congress Control Number: 2015948451

Edited by: Karen Li
Designed by: Barb Kelly

Canada Council for the Arts
Conseil des Arts du Canada

Canada

Manufactured in Shenzhen, China, in September 2015, by C&C Joint Printing Co.
Job #HP2932

A B C D E F

Publisher of Chirp, chickaDEE and OWL
www.owlkidsbooks.com

Owlkids Books is a division of

Frank and Laverne

BY DAVE WHAMOND AND JENNIFER STOKES
ILLUSTRATIONS BY DAVE WHAMOND

OWLKIDS BOOKS

SUNDAY

06:00 hours

Woke up and went outside for Squirrel Patrol.

Then I woke Laverne.

Laverne bunks in my house, too.

She's my friend.

We do basic training exercises together every day.

MONDAY
05:00 hours

Squirrel Patrol extra early this morning.

I like to be up with the humans as they get ready to go out.

They brush their teeth, comb their hair, and get dressed.

My job: to be underfoot.

My favorite human is Sam. His sister Molly is okay, too.

Sam is the oldest, and Molly is the youngest.

We're part of a pack.

I take Sam for a walk every day.
He likes to throw balls.

When I bring the ball back to him,
he throws it again.

Sometimes this can go on all afternoon.

Humans lead busy, exciting lives.
Dogs like me prefer the simple things:

A nice shoe
after a good meal.

The pure joy of barking.

And then, of course,
there's my favorite thing...
my stuffed fish, Eugene.

I've had him since I was a pup.

TUESDAY
08:00 hours

Late for Squirrel Patrol this morning.

Failed to report on time for duty after a bad night.

I just couldn't sleep.
I can't stop thinking about Carl, my next-door neighbor.

Carl's a Great Dane.
He's great all right —
great at being a bully!

I saw him charge at a little dog in the park yesterday.

He just better stay on his side of the fence!

I'll do whatever it takes
to protect Laverne and my humans.

Laverne and I spent some
R and R time together this afternoon.

She helped me take my mind off Carl.

She's such a good friend. 

WEDNESDAY

06:00 hours

Woke up the neighborhood with lots of barking — one of my many Squirrel Patrol duties.

ARF
YIP
YAP

Hee
Hee
Hee

Then spent the afternoon on Neighborhood Watch.

I take this very seriously.

My biggest job is to keep Carl under surveillance, so I got up on the chair for a better vantage point of the street.

Climbing on the furniture was a pretty daring maneuver, since I'm already on probation for that chewed-up rug incident.

I still don't know how the humans knew it was me...

THURSDAY
06:00 hours

Almost apprehended that squirrel this morning.

NUTS!

Afterward, Laverne tried to make me feel better.

But things went from bad to worse this afternoon.

Laverne was patrolling the backyard fence and got too close to Carl.

I could hear him jumping up and barking at her.

Thankfully, she got away!

Wish I could get over that fence and take care of Carl once and for all.

FRIDAY
06:00 hours

Squirrel Patrol at first light.

It was garbage day.

I LOVE garbage day —
the best smelling
day of the whole week.

Carl was sniffing down the street with his human.

Then, my worst nightmare:
Carl was approaching Sam and Molly
as they played in the front yard.

My humans were in danger!

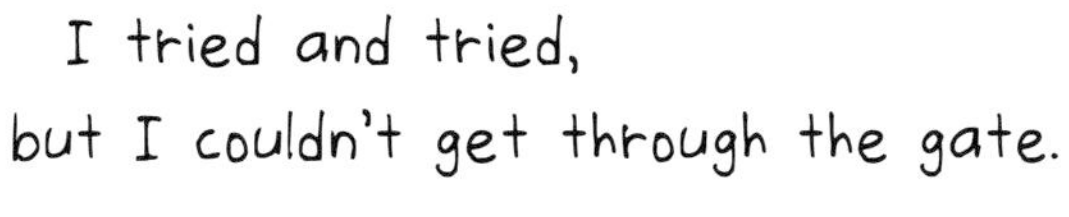

I tried and tried,
but I couldn't get through the gate.

Luckily, Sam and Molly were called in for lunch —
just in time!

Crisis averted.
But there's sure to be a next time...

SATURDAY
06:00 hours

Today started out the same as any other.

Then, just as that squirrel was about to escape
over the fence as usual,
we both realized...the gate was open!

The chase was on!

Until...

I ran into Carl.

I tried some evasive maneuvers.

But Carl was still hot on my tail.

Then guess who came to my rescue?

See why I love her soooo much?

Humans say that every dog has his day.
I think I just had mine.

Is that how it really happened? Close the book and flip it over for Laverne's side of the story!

Perhaps Frank has some redeeming qualities...

I'll have to sleep on it.

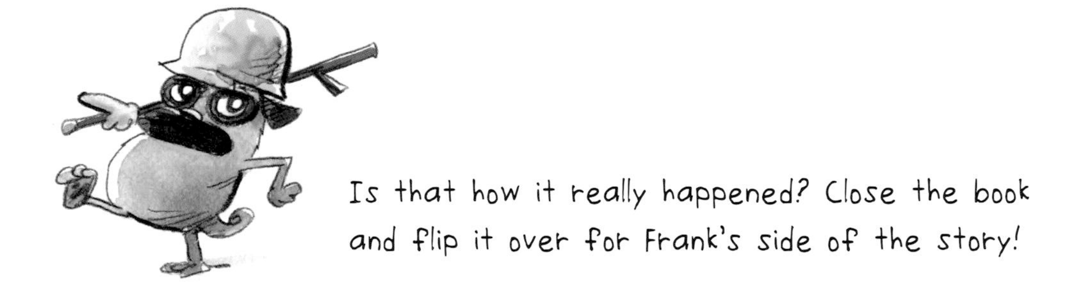

Is that how it really happened? Close the book and flip it over for Frank's side of the story!

Frank thinks I saved him.

He even left me
a thank-you present.

Then I realized those fleabags
were running in circles.

There were now *two* dogs in my yard!
This would not do.

Carl was hot on his tail,
and Frank ran as fast as his puny pug legs would let him.

This was *not* part of the plan —
but it was still working brilliantly!

SATURDAY

My plan worked flawlessly at first.

Frank shot out of the gate, delighted to be free.
I hoped he would run far, far away and never come back.

But then things got sticky.

What a commotion!
Frank was throwing himself at the gate,
trying to break it down.

That lunkhead hasn't a clue how to open it!

And then I had an idea...

an idea that would get
Frank out of my life forever!

FRIDAY

Garbage day. Revolting!
As expected, it's Frank's favorite day of the week.

I was sunning myself on the front balcony
when I noticed Carl sniffing his way
down the street with his human.

As Carl got close to Sam and Molly,
Frank naturally decided they were in mortal danger.

While I was taking my afternoon turn
along the backyard fence,
I was interrupted by two dogs
barking their heads off.

Frank thinks he's protecting me,
and Carl wants to play with me.

Honestly, I'm surrounded by dimwits.

THURSDAY

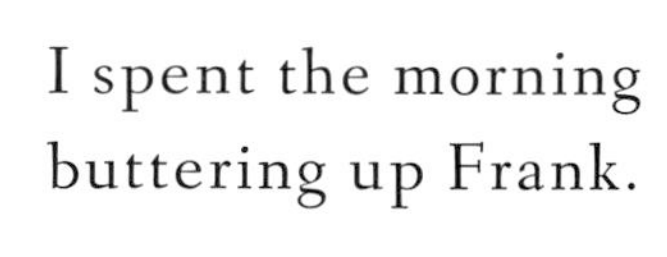

I spent the morning
buttering up Frank.

No luck.

He thinks I want to share that fish.

When the humans get home,
I'll direct their attention
to all those doggy hairs on
the furniture.

Maybe it will work as
well as that chewed-up
rug incident last week.

Maybe this time they'll send Frank away forever...

WEDNESDAY

Frank woke me with such
a racket this morning!

I'd been happily dreaming of muzzles.

He wasted all afternoon
on what he calls
Neighborhood Watch.

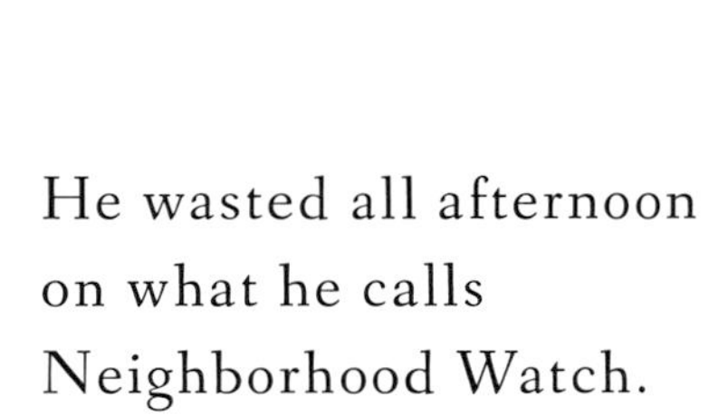

Who does he think
he's protecting?

Where was that fish?

I needed more information.

TUESDAY

What a terrible night!
Frank kept me awake till the wee hours,
circling around and around in his dog bed.

So I overslept this morning.
Luckily I woke up in time for my nap.

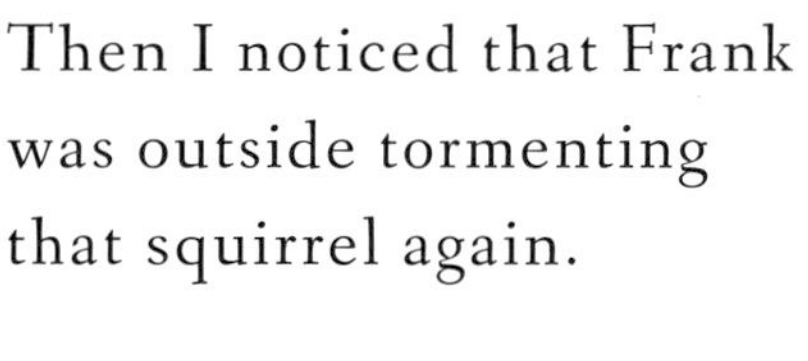

Then I noticed that Frank
was outside tormenting
that squirrel again.

This was my chance!

I save my energy
for essential things...

like getting Frank away from
his precious stuffed fish, Eugene,
before he chews it to tatters.

One day
that fish will be mine.

Unlike me, they don't understand
how to achieve a more refined quality of life:

Basking in sunlight.

Zen gardening.

Feline yoga.

The two big humans do
the most ridiculous things.

MONDAY

Frank woke me
extra early this morning.

I complained to the
humans with my own
wake-up call.

There are four humans
who live in my house.
If I had to choose a favorite, it
would be the medium-sized one, Sam.

He seems to understand me.

The littlest human
is Molly.

Her sole purpose is to cause me misery.

He's always bothering me
to play with him.

And you should
see the way he eats!

I give Frank daily lessons
on minding his manners.

SUNDAY

I was rudely awoken this morning.

I'm forced to share my house
with a creature the humans call FRANK.

He has no respect
for my morning schedule.

Frank *and* Laverne

BY DAVE WHAMOND AND JENNIFER STOKES
ILLUSTRATIONS BY DAVE WHAMOND

OWLKIDS BOOKS

Owlkids Books acknowledges the financial support of the Canada Council for the Arts, the Ontario Arts Council, the Government of Canada through the Canada Book Fund (CBF) and the Government of Ontario through the Ontario Media Development Corporation's Book Initiative for our publishing activities.

Published in Canada by
Owlkids Books Inc.
10 Lower Spadina Avenue
Toronto, ON M5V 2Z2

Published in the United States by
Owlkids Books Inc.
1700 Fourth Street
Berkeley, CA 94710

Library and Archives Canada Cataloguing in Publication

Whamond, Dave, author, illustrator
Frank and Laverne / by Dave Whamond and Jennifer Stokes ; illustrations by Dave Whamond.

Contents printed back-to-back and inverted.

ISBN 978-1-77147-145-9 (bound)

I. Stokes, Jennifer, author II. Title.

PS8645.H34F73 2016 jC813'.6 C2015-905420-6

Library of Congress Control Number: 2015948451

Edited by: Karen Li
Designed by: Barb Kelly

ONTARIO ARTS COUNCIL
CONSEIL DES ARTS DE L'ONTARIO
an Ontario government agency
un organisme du gouvernement de l'Ontario

Canada Council for the Arts
Conseil des Arts du Canada

Canada

Manufactured in Shenzhen, China, in September 2015, by C&C Joint Printing Co.
Job #HP2932

A B C D E F